The French Affair

Laurie Ravello

Published by Laurie Ravello, 2023.

THE FRENCH AFFAIR

First edition. September 20, 2023.

Copyright © 2023 Laurie Ravello.

ISBN: 979-8223211020

Written by Laurie Ravello.

Table of Contents

Dedicated to All

Romantics at Heart

Warm regards

Laurie Ravello

Author: Laurie Ravello

Laurie Ravello is an accomplished independent author celebrated for his exceptional talent in crafting stories that sweep readers off their feet and immerse them in the realms of love, romance, and profound discovery. With a remarkable ability to evoke powerful emotions and transport readers to captivating worlds, Laurie Ravello has become a literary force to be reckoned with.

Throughout his writing career, Laurie Ravello has demonstrated an innate gift for weaving intricate tales of love and romance that resonate deeply with readers. His narratives are known for their ability to take readers on emotional journeys, introducing them to characters whose experiences are both relatable and profoundly moving.

Laurie Ravello's works have earned acclaim for their vivid storytelling, rich character development, and the ability to explore the complexities of human emotions. Whether it's a tender love story, a passionate romance, or a narrative of self-discovery, Ravello's writing shines with authenticity and depth.

As an independent author, Laurie Ravello's dedication to his craft is evident in the way he meticulously constructs his stories. His narratives are often accompanied by beautifully descriptive prose that paints a vivid picture of the worlds he creates, allowing readers to fully immerse themselves in the story's settings and atmospheres.

With each new release, Laurie Ravello continues to captivate readers and earn their loyalty with his talent for crafting tales that touch the heart and soul. His work serves as an invitation to embark on journeys of love, passion, and self-discovery, leaving readers eagerly anticipating his next literary adventure.

Laurie Ravello's commitment to his craft and his ability to transport readers into the depths of love and romance have firmly established him as an independent author whose stories are cherished by those seeking narratives that both stir the emotions and provide an unforgettable literary experience.

Warm Regards
Laurie Ravello

Title: The French Affair

Synopsis: "The French Affair"

In "The French Affair," readers are invited into the enchanting world of Tristan Orton, a London musician, and Marie-Élise, a talented artist from Paris. Their love story unfolds against the backdrop of France, weaving together the mesmerizing realms of music, art, and an unbreakable bond that defies time itself.

Tristan, a gifted guitarist, embarks on a soul-searching journey to France, seeking inspiration for his music. It is within the romantic streets of Paris that he encounters Marie-Élise, a captivating artist showcasing her paintings in one of the city's most renowned galleries. Their initial meeting sparks a profound connection that transcends language and logic, setting the stage for an epic romance.

As their love story blooms, readers are transported to the heart of France, with its picturesque landscapes, charming avenues, and the alluring allure of the City of Love, Paris. The narrative is rich with sensory descriptions, inviting readers to savour the flavours, sounds, and ambiance of this captivating setting.

The novel follows Tristan and Marie-Élise's journey from the romantic streets of Paris to their new home in Vienna, Austria, where they build a life intertwined with creativity, family, and an enduring devotion to their respective arts. Over the course of 35 chapters, readers bear witness to the evolution of their love, the trials they face, and the profound impact they have on each other's lives.

"The French Affair" celebrates the enduring power of love, artistic expression, and the timeless nature of genuine passion. It explores themes of dedication, artistic pursuit, and the profound influence that love can exert over one's life. The beautifully crafted prose and intricately developed characters invite readers to embark on an emotional and transformative journey that culminates in a poignant and unforgettable conclusion.

This heartfelt and evocative novel is an homage to the capacity of love to transcend boundaries, leaving an indelible mark on the hearts of those who dare to believe in the enchantment of a love that endures through time and distance.

Introduction:

In the heart of this narrative lies a tale as timeless as love itself, where the world becomes a canvas and the notes of passion paint the very air. "The French Affair" invites you to embark on a journey through the vibrant streets of Paris and the enchanting melodies of Vienna, where two souls, Tristan Orton, a London musician, and Marie-Élise, a gifted artist from Paris, discover that destiny often orchestrates the most beautiful symphonies.

Set against a backdrop of artistic brilliance and the romance of two iconic European cities, this story transcends the boundaries of time and space to explore the profound depths of human connection. It is a narrative that weaves together the threads of love, artistry, and self-discovery, inviting readers to immerse themselves in a world where every brushstroke and every note played tells a story of passion, creativity, and the enduring power of a love that defies all odds.

Join us as we venture into the intricacies of their love story, where the streets of Paris and the quiet alleys of Vienna bear witness to a romance that is destined to leave an indelible mark on your heart. "The French Affair" is not merely a story; it is a symphony of emotions, a canvas of vivid experiences, and an invitation to believe in the magic of love and artistry—a love that knows no borders and an artistry that transcends time.

Chapter 1: A Journey to France's Heart

Tristan Orton gazed out of the airplane window, his heart quickening with anticipation as the vast landscape of France stretched beneath him. The first glimpse of the French countryside was like stepping into a masterpiece of nature, a canvas painted with the most vibrant and delicate strokes.

The rolling hills unfolded beneath him, their contours a mesmerizing dance of light and shadow. These hills, adorned with a patchwork quilt of emerald green vineyards, stretched to the horizon, each row of grapevines standing at attention, their leaves rustling softly in the breeze. The golden rays of the setting sun bathed the landscape in a warm, ethereal glow, casting long, romantic shadows that seemed to caress the land.

As the plane descended further, Tristan's eyes were drawn to endless fields of lavender, their violet blooms a testament to the beauty of nature's artistry. The air was perfumed with the sweet, intoxicating scent of the flowers, a fragrant welcome to the land of romance. He imagined walking through those fields, the lavender brushing against his fingertips as he lost himself in their serene beauty.

The French countryside was a tapestry of life, crisscrossed with meandering rivers and streams, their crystal-clear waters reflecting the azure sky above. Tristan watched as a small wooden bridge spanned one such waterway, leading to a charming stone cottage nestled amid a grove of ancient olive trees. The scene was so picturesque that it felt as if he had stepped into the pages of a fairy tale.

The villages that dotted the landscape were like gems, their terracotta rooftops basking in the sun's warm embrace. The buildings were adorned with colourful shutters, and narrow cobblestone streets wound through the heart of each village, inviting exploration. Tristan could imagine the laughter of children playing in the streets and the scent of freshly baked bread wafting from the local boulangerie.

The plane's descent brought Tristan closer to the heart of France, and he marvelled at fields of sunflowers that stretched as far as the eye could see. The sunflowers stood tall and proud, their golden heads turning to follow the path of the sun, like a cheerful chorus singing the praises of this enchanting land. Each bloom seemed to radiate its own unique personality, adding to the symphony of colour and life that surrounded him.

Finally, as the plane approached Paris, the City of Love, Tristan's heart swelled with awe. The Eiffel Tower stood tall, its iron lattice reaching for the heavens, while the Seine River wound its way through the heart of the city, lined with centuries-old buildings that told stories of a romantic past. Tristan couldn't help but be overwhelmed by the sheer beauty of France's countryside, a breath taking introduction to a journey that promised not only artistic inspiration but also the possibility of a love story as magnificent as the landscape itself. With a deep breath, he knew that his adventure in this land of dreams had only just begun.

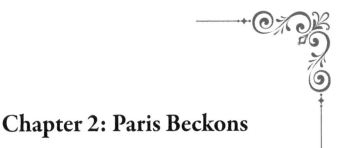

Chapter 2: Paris Beckons

The plane touched down at Charles de Gaulle Airport, and Tristan felt a surge of excitement as he stepped onto French soil. The airport buzzed with the energy of travellers from around the world, each person carrying their own hopes and dreams. For Tristan, it was the dream of finding inspiration in the heart of Paris, a city that had beckoned to artists and dreamers for centuries.

As he made his way through the bustling airport, Tristan couldn't help but notice the elegant style of the French. Women with impeccable fashion sense strolled past, effortlessly chic in their attire. Men in well-tailored suits exuded an air of confidence. It was a city where style was not just a choice but a way of life.

Navigating the airport, Tristan's thoughts turned to his decision to take this journey. London had been his home for years, and while he loved the city's vibrant music scene, he had felt a creative stagnation creeping in. His songs had become predictable, lacking the spark of inspiration that had once fuelled his music. France, with its rich history of art and romance, seemed like the perfect antidote.

Outside the airport, Tristan hailed a taxi, and as he gazed out of the window, the streets of Paris unfolded before him. The city was a tapestry of architectural wonders, a seamless blend of the past and the present. Grand boulevards stretched as far as the eye could see, lined with elegant Haussmannian buildings adorned with intricate wrought-iron balconies. The charm of Paris was not just in its landmarks but in its every street corner, where history whispered through the cobblestones.

Tristan's destination was a small boutique hotel tucked away in the heart of the city, a place he had carefully chosen for its proximity to the artistic soul of Paris. As he checked into his room, he couldn't help but feel a sense of exhilaration. The adventure had begun, and he was ready to immerse himself in the city's culture and creativity.

That evening, Tristan ventured out to explore the streets of Paris. The city was a sensory delight, with the aroma of freshly baked baguettes drifting from quaint bakeries, the sound of musicians serenading passers-by, and the soft glow of streetlights casting a romantic ambiance. He found himself at a bustling café, savouring a glass of red wine and watching as people strolled by, lost in their own stories.

As the night deepened, Tristan's thoughts turned to the reason for his journey—a quest for artistic inspiration that would breathe new life into his music. He knew that in the days to come, he would seek out the galleries, the music venues, and the hidden corners of Paris where creativity thrived. And perhaps, in this city of dreams, he would discover not only his muse but also a love story as enchanting as the Parisian nights.

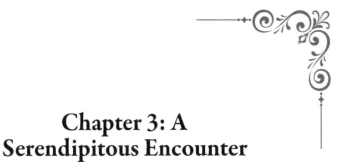

Chapter 3: A Serendipitous Encounter

The days in Paris began to take on a rhythm of their own for Tristan. Each morning, he would wake up to the soft melody of a distant accordion playing in the streets below, and the aroma of freshly brewed coffee wafting through the open windows of his boutique hotel room. The city's charm was working its magic on him, filling his senses and infusing his soul with a renewed sense of purpose.

One sunny morning, Tristan decided to visit the Musée d'Orsay, a treasure trove of Impressionist masterpieces. As he wandered through the galleries, he was captivated by the strokes of Monet, the vibrant colours of Renoir, and the emotional depth of Van Gogh's paintings. It was as though he had stepped into a world where emotions flowed freely, and every brushstroke told a story.

Outside the museum, he strolled along the Seine River, where artists had set up their easels, capturing the essence of Paris on canvas. The riverbanks were alive with creativity, a testament to the city's enduring allure for artists of all kinds. Tristan admired their work, wondering if, in some small way, he could leave his own mark on this artistic tapestry.

It was during one of these leisurely walks that he stumbled upon a charming art studio nestled in a cobblestone alley. The door stood invitingly ajar, and a soft melody emanated from within. Tristan's curiosity got the better of him, and he pushed the door open.

Inside, the studio was a riot of colours and creativity. Canvases leaned against walls, each one telling a unique story, and an assortment of paintbrushes and palettes lay scattered on a worn wooden table. At the centre of it all was Marie-Élise, her fiery hair cascading over her shoulders as she swayed to the music, her hand moving rhythmically across a canvas. Her eyes, a captivating shade of green, were filled with a deep, almost ethereal, concentration.

For a moment, Tristan simply watched, entranced by the artist at work. The air in the studio was thick with the scent of paint, a heady mix of earthy hues and vibrant pigments. It was a scent that spoke of creation and expression, a language he was eager to learn.

Marie-Élise must have sensed his presence, for she turned, her eyes widening in surprise. A streak of cobalt blue paint adorned her cheek, and her lips curved into a warm, welcoming smile. In that instant, Tristan felt a connection, as though fate had led him to this serendipitous encounter.

She gestured for him to come closer, and Tristan stepped into the studio, his heart pounding with a mixture of nerves and excitement. He introduced himself, and as they spoke, he discovered that Marie-Élise was not only a talented artist but also a kindred spirit. She shared her passion for art, her love for Paris, and the story behind each painting.

As the hours slipped away in conversation and shared laughter, Tristan couldn't help but feel that he had stumbled upon something extraordinary. In this small art studio in the heart of Paris, he had found not only inspiration but also the possibility of a connection that transcended the boundaries of art and music. Little did he know that their meeting was the beginning of a journey that would change both their lives forever?

Chapter 4: The Colours of Connection

Days turned into weeks as Tristan and Marie-Élise's connection deepened. The art studio became their sanctuary, a place where their creative energies intertwined, sparking inspiration and forging a bond that defied easy description. As they painted and played music side by side, it felt as though their souls communicated through the language of art.

The canvas Tristan had brought with him from London took on a life of its own under Marie-Élise's guidance. Together, they created a masterpiece that merged Tristan's musical passion with Marie-Élise's visual artistry. It was a testament to their collaboration, a testament to the unspoken understanding that had blossomed between them.

One evening, as the sun dipped below the horizon, painting the Parisian sky with hues of orange and pink, they shared a quiet dinner at a charming bistro tucked away in Montmartre. The tables spilled onto the cobbled streets, and the atmosphere was alive with laughter and music. Tristan couldn't help but feel that he was living in a dream, one where every moment was imbued with a sense of wonder.

Their conversations ranged from art to music, dreams to fears, and everything in between. Marie-Élise spoke of her journey as an artist, the challenges she had faced, and the joy she found in creation. Tristan shared his own struggles as a musician and his quest for a new sound, one that would capture the essence of his time in Paris.

As the night grew darker, they strolled to the Place du Tertre, where artists had gathered for centuries to display their work. The square was a kaleidoscope of colours and creativity, with painters, musicians, and poets all vying for the attention of passers-by. Tristan watched as Marie-Élise's eyes lit up with passion, her admiration for her fellow artists evident.

It was there, beneath the starlit sky of Montmartre, that Tristan realized how deeply he had fallen for Marie-Élise. Her spirit, her talent, and the way she saw the world had captured his heart. He took her hand, his fingers entwining with hers, and whispered words of admiration and affection. In that moment, beneath the watchful gaze of the artists who had come before them, they shared their first kiss—a sweet, electric spark that sealed their love.

From that night on, Tristan and Marie-Élise's relationship blossomed into a full-blown romance, a love story that echoed the passion and creativity of Paris itself. They ventured further into the city's hidden corners, discovering its secret gardens, cosy cafés, and the enchanting beauty of its neighbourhoods.

But amidst the magic of Paris, challenges loomed on the horizon. Their love was a symphony of colours, but like any masterpiece, it faced moments of uncertainty and doubt. As they navigated the complexities of their own lives and the expectations of the world around them, they would come to realize that true love, like art, required patience, understanding, and the willingness to embrace both the light and the shadows.

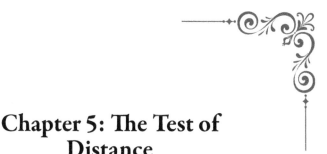

Chapter 5: The Test of Distance

The days in Paris passed in a whirlwind of love and creativity for Tristan and Marie-Élise. Their love was a passionate crescendo, a symphony of emotions that echoed through the City of Light. But as the weeks turned into months, a looming challenge cast a shadow over their blossoming romance—the inevitability of distance.

Tristan's time in Paris was coming to an end, and he had to return to London to fulfil his musical commitments. The prospect of leaving Marie-Élise behind was a bittersweet melody that played in his heart. They spent their final days together savouring every moment, as if trying to capture time itself.

On their last night in Paris, they visited the Eiffel Tower, where they stood at its summit, gazing out at the city's glittering lights. Tristan held Marie-Élise close, his heart heavy with the knowledge that they would soon be separated by miles and borders. They made promises to each other, vows of love and devotion, and pledged to overcome the challenges that lay ahead.

Back in London, Tristan returned to the world of music, but his heart remained in Paris. The city's influence was evident in his compositions, which now carried the essence of the romance and beauty he had discovered in the City of Light. He often found himself longing for the cobblestone streets, the aroma of freshly baked croissants, and most of all, the presence of Marie-Élise.

Distance tested their love, but Tristan and Marie-Élise were determined to make it work. They exchanged handwritten letters, each one a testament to their longing and commitment. Tristan's music became a bridge that connected them, and he composed songs inspired by his love for Marie-Élise, sending them as heartfelt serenades across the miles.

Marie-Élise, too, continued to create, her paintings reflecting the emotions and memories of their time together. In her studio, she would lose herself in her art, finding solace in the strokes of her brushes and the vivid colours of her canvases. Their shared passion for creation was a lifeline that kept their love strong.

But as the months passed, the ache of separation grew. Tristan missed the feel of Marie-Élise's hand in his, the way she laughed, and the warmth of her presence. It was a longing that couldn't be eased by letters or phone calls, a yearning for the tangible connection they once shared.

One day, Tristan received an unexpected invitation to attend an art exhibition in London. It was an event featuring Marie-Élise's work, and she had secretly arranged for her paintings to be displayed in his city. It was a poignant gesture, a way to bridge the distance and create a tangible link between their worlds.

The night of the exhibition, Tristan stood before Marie-Élise's paintings, each one a reflection of their love story. As he gazed at her art, he felt a sense of awe and gratitude. It was a reminder that their love, like art itself, transcended the boundaries of time and space. And as they stood together in the heart of London, their love story continued to evolve, proving that distance could never truly extinguish the flame of their passion.

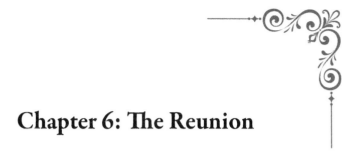

Chapter 6: The Reunion

The months stretched into a year of separation, and the ache in Tristan's heart grew with each passing day. He had continued to compose music, finding solace in the melodies that reminded him of Marie-Élise. But it was an empty kind of solace, one that only deepened his longing for her.

One evening, as he was playing a hauntingly beautiful melody on his guitar, the doorbell of his London apartment rang. Startled, he set aside his guitar and made his way to the door. He had not been expecting any visitors, and his heart quickened with curiosity.

As he opened the door, a wave of disbelief washed over him. Standing before him, her fiery hair cascading around her shoulders, was Marie-Élise. She wore a bright smile that lit up the room, and in her arms, she held a canvas covered in a cloth.

Without a word, Tristan pulled her into a tight embrace, as if trying to convince himself that she was real. The sensation of her in his arms, the scent of her hair, and the sound of her laughter were overwhelming in their intensity. It was a reunion he had dreamt of countless times, but one he had begun to fear might never happen.

Marie-Élise explained that she had managed to secure a temporary residency in London, a chance to be closer to Tristan and rekindle their love. The canvas she held was a gift, a painting she had created during her time apart, a testament to the strength of their connection.

Over the following days, Tristan and Marie-Élise embarked on a journey of rediscovery. London, with its bustling streets and historic landmarks, became the backdrop for their rekindled romance. They visited the iconic Abbey Road, walked along the serene banks of the Thames, and explored the hidden corners of the city, holding hands and sharing stolen kisses.

Tristan's London apartment, once a place of solitude and longing, was transformed into a haven of love and creativity. The canvas Marie-Élise had brought with her became a collaborative masterpiece, a symbol of their shared passion and the depth of their connection. Each brushstroke was a declaration of their love, and every color on the canvas held a story of their journey.

As the days turned into weeks, Tristan and Marie-Élise's love story continued to evolve. They faced the challenges of blending their lives, learning to navigate the intricacies of a shared future. There were moments of doubt and uncertainty, but their love remained steadfast, a force that could weather any storm.

Their reunion in London was a testament to the enduring power of love, a reminder that distance could be overcome, and that the heart could find its way back to where it truly belonged. Tristan and Marie-Élise had learned that love was not just a fleeting emotion but a choice, a commitment to cherish and nurture the connection they had found in the most unexpected of places.

As they stood before their collaborative masterpiece, surrounded by the melodies of their intertwined hearts, they knew that their love story was far from over. It was a story that would continue to unfold, painting the canvas of their lives with the vibrant colours of passion, creativity, and an enduring love that had weathered the test of time and distance.

Chapter 7: A Love Rekindled

With Marie-Élise's presence in London, Tristan's life had transformed into a vibrant tapestry of shared experiences and newfound dreams. The city that had once felt like a solitary backdrop to his music was now alive with the colours of their love story. Together, they embarked on a journey of rekindling their romance, savouring every moment as if it were a precious work of art.

Their days were filled with adventures that spanned both old and new, as they explored London's iconic landmarks and uncovered hidden gems. They strolled through Hyde Park, picnicking beneath the shade of ancient trees, and visited the historic British Museum, where they marvelled at the world's treasures.

In the evenings, they often dined at cosy restaurants, indulging in culinary delights from around the world. The candlelit dinners were moments of intimacy, where they shared their dreams and aspirations, deepening their connection and strengthening their bond.

But it was the music that truly brought them closer. Tristan and Marie-Élise would spend hours in his apartment, their instruments and voices harmonizing in a beautiful symphony of love. Tristan's guitar and Marie-Élise's ethereal vocals blended together seamlessly, creating melodies that resonated with the depth of their emotions.

One evening, as they sat on the balcony of Tristan's apartment, the London skyline spread out before them, painted in hues of orange and pink by the setting sun. Tristan strummed his guitar, and Marie-Élise's voice filled the air with a hauntingly beautiful melody. It was a song of love and longing, a song that captured the essence of their journey.

As they finished the song, Tristan set aside his guitar and turned to Marie-Élise. With a tender smile, he spoke from his heart, expressing the depth of his love and his desire to spend the rest of his life with her. Marie-Élise's eyes glistened with tears of joy as she responded with a heartfelt "yes," sealing their commitment to each other.

Their engagement was a celebration of their enduring love and the promise of a future filled with shared dreams. They began making plans for a life together, blending their artistic passions and envisioning a world where their creativity would flourish in harmony.

But amidst the joy of their engagement, there were moments of reflection. They knew that their love had weathered the challenges of distance and uncertainty, but there were still obstacles to overcome. Questions of where to call home and how to merge their artistic pursuits loomed on the horizon, casting shadows of doubt.

Yet, Tristan and Marie-Élise were determined to face these challenges together, with the same unwavering commitment that had carried them through their separation. Their love had been rekindled in the most beautiful of ways, and they knew that it was a flame that could withstand anything.

As they held each other in the fading light of the London evening, they were filled with hope and anticipation for the next chapter of their love story. It was a story that had unfolded against the backdrop of art and music, a story that had seen its share of trials and triumphs, and a story that was bound to be an enduring masterpiece, painted with the colours of their hearts.

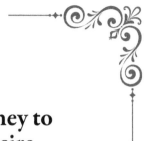

Chapter 8: A Journey to Their Heart's Desire

With their engagement, Tristan and Marie-Élise embarked on a journey that would lead them to their heart's deepest desires. They faced the challenges that came with blending their lives, dreams, and artistic pursuits with unwavering determination.

The question of where to call home remained a central theme in their journey. London held Tristan's roots as a musician, and it was where their love had rekindled. Paris, on the other hand, was Marie-Élise's artistic haven, the place where her heart had found its muse. They spent long nights discussing the possibilities, weighing the pros and cons, and searching for a compromise that would allow them to thrive as individuals and as a couple.

Amidst the uncertainty, they found solace in their creative pursuits. Tristan and Marie-Élise continued to collaborate on music and art, drawing inspiration from their shared experiences and the love that bound them together. Their work resonated with a unique depth, a reflection of the passion and devotion they poured into their crafts.

The months passed, and they decided to split their time between London and Paris, allowing them to nurture their respective careers while being together as a couple. It was a solution that required sacrifice and adaptability, but they were willing to make it work for the sake of their love.

In London, they attended music festivals and art exhibitions, sharing their talents with the world. In Paris, they wandered through the romantic streets, finding inspiration in the city's artistic atmosphere. Their love story became an inspiration to others, a testament to the power of love and the pursuit of one's passions.

But as they navigated the complexities of their dual-city life, they encountered challenges they had not anticipated. The distance, even within the same continent, could be a strain on their relationship. There were moments of loneliness and doubt, but they were always followed by a reaffirmation of their love.

It was during one such moment of doubt that Tristan composed a heartfelt song, a love letter to Marie-Élise. He performed it for her in their London apartment, pouring his emotions into every note and lyric. The song captured the essence of their journey—the longing, the devotion, and the unwavering belief in their love.

As the final chords of the song resonated in the room, Tristan looked into Marie-Élise's eyes, his heart laid bare before her. In that moment, they both knew that their love was worth every sacrifice, every challenge, and every uncertainty. Their journey to their heart's desire was ongoing, but it was a journey they were willing to take together, hand in hand, creating a life filled with art, music, and an enduring love that had overcome every obstacle in its path.

Chapter 9: A Tale of Two Cities

Tristan and Marie-Élise's life split between London and Paris brought those moments of both beauty and complexity. They had learned to navigate the intricacies of a dual-city existence, but challenges still lay ahead. Each time they said goodbye at the train station or the airport, their hearts ached with the weight of separation, even if it was for a short time.

In London, Tristan continued to compose music, drawing inspiration from the city's vibrant music scene. He played at local venues, sharing his melodies with an ever-growing audience. His songs, inspired by his love for Marie-Élise, resonated deeply with listeners, and he began to gain recognition as an artist.

Marie-Élise, on the other hand, thrived in Paris, where she exhibited her paintings in prestigious galleries and continued to create breath-taking art that captured the essence of the city. Her talent and dedication to her craft earned her acclaim in the art world, and her work was sought after by collectors.

But their time apart was not without its moments of doubt and loneliness. Late-night phone calls and video chats could never fully replace the warmth of their physical presence. The time zones and the demands of their careers often left them yearning for more time together.

Yet, every reunion was a celebration, a reminder of the love that had transcended borders and distance. They explored new corners of London and Paris together, seeking out hidden gems and creating cherished memories. Their love remained as passionate as ever, fuelled by the knowledge that they were each other's muse and anchor.

Tristan's apartment in London and Marie-Élise's studio in Paris became their sanctuaries, places where they could escape the demands of the world and immerse themselves in their shared passion for art and music. The canvases and instruments that filled their spaces were witnesses to the depths of their creativity and the strength of their connection.

As they continued to walk the tightrope between two cities, they knew that the challenges they faced were a small price to pay for a love as extraordinary as theirs. The moments of separation only made their reunions sweeter, and their love story continued to evolve, a tale of two cities and two hearts bound together by a love that knew no bounds.

Chapter 10: The Art of Compromise

As the seasons turned and the years passed, Tristan and Marie-Élise's love story had woven a rich tapestry, intricately blending two lives, two cities, and two artistic souls. They had faced the challenges of their dual-city existence with unwavering determination, but the time had come to seek a more permanent solution to their life together.

The question of where to establish their home had loomed large for years. London and Paris held special places in their hearts, and each city had shaped their identities as artists. They knew that they could not simply choose one over the other without sacrificing a part of themselves.

In their search for a solution, they explored new possibilities. They considered a third city, one that could serve as a neutral ground where they could both pursue their creative passions. They travelled together to different European cities, hoping to find a place that resonated with both of them.

One such journey took them to Vienna, a city steeped in history, art, and music. As they walked through the streets, they felt a sense of harmony, as if the city itself embraced their love story. Vienna offered a vibrant arts scene, with galleries, concert halls, and cultural events that spoke to their artistic souls.

In Vienna, they discovered a charming apartment with high ceilings, large windows, and space for both Tristan's music studio and Marie-Élise's art studio. It was a place that felt like a blank canvas, ready to be filled with the colours of their love and creativity.

With a sense of excitement and anticipation, they made the decision to establish Vienna as their new home. It was a compromise that allowed them to continue pursuing their artistic dreams while creating a life together. They sold their apartments in London and Paris, bidding farewell to the cities that had played such significant roles in their love story.

The move to Vienna was a fresh beginning, a chapter in their love story that held the promise of new adventures and shared dreams. They found themselves immersed in the city's artistic and cultural scene, attending concerts, exhibitions, and exploring the city's historic sites hand in hand.

In their new home, Tristan and Marie-Élise continued to collaborate on projects that blended music and art, creating works that were a reflection of their deep connection. Vienna became not only the backdrop but also an integral part of their love story, a place where their creativity flourished.

Their journey had been one of compromise and adaptability, a testament to the strength of their love. They had learned that love was not about finding the perfect place or the perfect circumstances but about finding the perfect person to share life's joys and challenges. In Vienna, they had found a harmonious melody that resonated with their hearts, a place where their love story could continue to evolve, a timeless masterpiece painted with the colours of their souls.

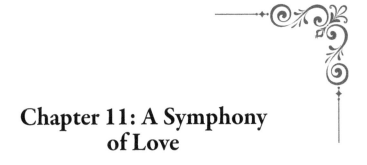

Chapter 11: A Symphony of Love

In the heart of Vienna, Tristan and Marie-Élise's love story continued to flourish, their lives interwoven like a harmonious symphony. Their decision to establish a new home had brought them a sense of stability and the freedom to fully embrace their creative passions.

Their Vienna apartment had become a sanctuary of art and music. Tristan's guitars lined one corner of the living room, while Marie-Élise's canvases and easels filled another. It was a space where their creativity flowed freely, a testament to the depth of their connection.

In this new chapter of their love story, they continued to collaborate on projects that merged their artistic talents. Tristan composed music inspired by Marie-Élise's paintings, and Marie-Élise created artworks that captured the essence of Tristan's melodies. Their work resonated with audiences, evoking emotions and connections that transcended language.

Vienna itself served as a wellspring of inspiration. The city's rich history of classical music and art was a source of motivation for Tristan and Marie-Élise. They attended concerts at iconic venues like the Vienna State Opera and explored museums that held treasures from centuries past. Vienna's grandeur and artistic heritage became an integral part of their creative journey.

Their love, too, continued to deepen. Tristan and Marie-Élise's shared dreams and experiences strengthened their bond, and their connection remained as passionate as the day they had rekindled their love in Paris. They celebrated milestones together, from anniversaries of their engagement to the successful exhibitions of Marie-Élise's artwork.

But they also faced the challenges that life inevitably brought. Tristan's music career took him on tours, and Marie-Élise encountered periods of creative blocks. In those moments, their love was tested, and they learned the importance of patience, understanding, and unwavering support.

One evening, as they stood on their apartment balcony, looking out at the illuminated city of Vienna, Tristan took Marie-Élise's hand in his and spoke from the depths of his heart. He expressed his gratitude for the life they had built together, the love that had carried them through every obstacle, and the dreams they had yet to fulfil.

Marie-Élise smiled, her eyes filled with love and tenderness, and she shared her own dreams and hopes for their future. It was a moment of profound connection, a reaffirmation of their commitment to each other and to their shared journey.

As the years passed, Tristan and Marie-Élise's love story became a testament to the enduring power of love and creativity. They had learned that love was not about finding the perfect place or the perfect circumstances but about finding the perfect person to share life's joys and challenges. In Vienna, they had discovered the harmony of their souls, a place where their love story continued to evolve, a timeless masterpiece painted with the colours of their hearts, a symphony of love that would echo through the ages.

Chapter 12: The Journey Continues

The years rolled on, and Tristan and Marie-Élise's life in Vienna had blossomed into a harmonious symphony of love and creativity. Their story was a testament to the enduring power of passion, resilience, and a love that knew no bounds. But as time flowed, new chapters unfolded, and their journey continued to evolve.

Tristan's music career had reached new heights, and he had garnered a dedicated global following. His songs, infused with the emotions of his love for Marie-Élise, resonated deeply with listeners from all corners of the world. His tours took him to far-flung places, and Marie-Élise often accompanied him, turning their travels into adventures filled with inspiration and discovery.

Marie-Élise's art had also flourished, and her exhibitions in Vienna and beyond had gained recognition in the international art scene. Her paintings continued to captivate viewers, evoking a sense of wonder and emotion. Her work had evolved, reflecting the changing seasons of their love, and her canvases had become windows to their shared journey.

In the midst of their artistic successes, Tristan and Marie-Élise had another dream they longed to fulfil—a family of their own. They had always known that parenthood was a part of their love story waiting to be written. After years of trying, their dream came true, and they welcomed a child into their lives, a symbol of their love and commitment.

Becoming parents brought a new depth to their love. The sleepless nights, the laughter of their child, and the shared moments of wonder and joy bound them even closer together. Parenthood, like their artistic endeavours, was a collaboration, and they navigated its challenges with the same unwavering love and support that had carried them through the years.

As their child grew, Tristan and Marie-Élise continued to balance their creative careers with the joys of family life. Vienna remained their home, a place where their love had flourished, and they remained deeply connected to the city's cultural and artistic heritage.

But amidst the busyness of their lives, they made a promise to each other—a promise to keep nurturing their love story. They set aside time for quiet moments together, whether it was sharing a meal, playing music, or simply strolling through Vienna's picturesque streets hand in hand. Their love, like a fine wine, had only grown richer with time.

Their journey was a testament to the power of compromise, communication, and a love that embraced every challenge and triumph. They had learned that love was not just a destination but a journey, one that continued to unfold with every passing day.

And so, Tristan and Marie-Élise's love story continued, a story that had begun in the romantic streets of Paris, had thrived in the vibrant cities of London and Vienna, and had evolved with the changing seasons of their lives. It was a story of passion, creativity, and an enduring love that had stood the test of time, a story that would continue to inspire and captivate, echoing through the ages.

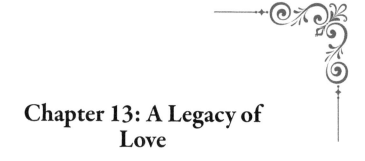

Chapter 13: A Legacy of Love

The passing years had transformed Tristan and Marie-Élise's love story into a tapestry of shared experiences, enduring devotion, and artistic brilliance. As they entered the autumn of their lives, they reflected on the chapters that had led them to this moment—a moment where their love had deepened and evolved into a legacy that would outlast them.

Their child had grown into a remarkable individual, inheriting their love for music and art. The family's Vienna apartment had witnessed countless jam sessions, artistic collaborations, and moments of laughter and connection. Tristan and Marie-Élise had nurtured their child's talents, instilling in them the values of creativity, passion, and the importance of pursuing one's dreams.

Vienna, with its historic charm and cultural richness, had remained their anchor. Their love for the city had only grown stronger over the years, and they had become part of its artistic fabric. They had attended countless concerts, exhibitions, and cultural events, contributing their own art to the vibrant tapestry of Vienna's cultural scene.

Tristan's music had continued to resonate with audiences of all ages, and his songs had become timeless classics. He had released albums inspired by his love story with Marie-Élise, and his music had become a source of inspiration for generations. His concerts, often featuring Marie-Élise's artwork as a backdrop, were a testament to their enduring collaboration.

Marie-Élise's paintings had evolved with time, each canvas a reflection of the seasons of their love and the beauty of the world around them. Her art had touched the hearts of art enthusiasts worldwide, and her legacy as a visionary artist was firmly established. She had continued to experiment with new techniques and styles, pushing the boundaries of her creativity.

As they looked back on their life together, Tristan and Marie-Élise marvelled at the journey they had undertaken. Their love had transcended time, distance, and challenges, and it had grown into a legacy that extended far beyond themselves. Their love story had become a source of inspiration, a reminder that true love could weather any storm and flourish amidst the complexities of life.

In the twilight of their years, Tristan and Marie-Élise knew that their love was a gift—a gift that had enriched their lives, touched the lives of others, and left an indelible mark on the world. They felt a profound sense of gratitude for the love they had shared, the art they had created, and the family they had nurtured.

And so, as they embraced the present moment and looked ahead to the future, they were filled with a deep contentment. Their love story had evolved into a legacy of love, a testament to the power of passion, creativity, and the enduring bond between two souls who had found their muse in each other. It was a legacy that would live on, inspiring generations to come, echoing through time as a testament to the enduring power of love.

Chapter 14: The Final Movement

As Tristan and Marie-Élise reached the pinnacle of their lives together, they were acutely aware that their time on this Earth was finite. Their love story, which had spanned decades and had been a source of inspiration and beauty, was approaching its final movement. It was a chapter they had both anticipated with a mixture of reflection and acceptance.

They had shared a lifetime of memories, from the romantic streets of Paris to the vibrant scenes of London and the cultural riches of Vienna. Their love had grown deeper with each passing year, their bond unbreakable, and their artistic collaboration had left an indelible mark on the world.

As they aged, Tristan's fingers found it more challenging to pluck the strings of his guitar, and Marie-Élise's hand trembled slightly as she held her brushes. But their creativity never waned. They continued to create, albeit at a slower pace, finding solace in their art and the shared moments of inspiration that had defined their love.

Their child had grown into a successful artist and musician in their own right, a testament to the values and talents they had instilled. They now had a family legacy of creativity and love that would continue to flourish and inspire future generations.

Tristan and Marie-Élise had seen their love story transform into a legacy, one that had touched countless hearts around the world. Their art and music had transcended time and place, becoming a source of inspiration for those who had followed their journey.

As they faced the inevitable conclusion of their love story, they did so with grace and gratitude. They had lived a life filled with passion, creativity, and a love that had endured every trial. Their love had been a gift, one that had enriched their lives and the lives of others, and they cherished every moment they had shared.

In the quiet moments of their final days together, they held hands, their fingers intertwined like the chords of a timeless melody. They shared stories of their journey, recalling the beauty of their love story and the moments that had defined their lives.

And as they gazed into each other's eyes, they knew that their love, like a well-composed symphony, would continue to resonate in the hearts of those who had been touched by their art, their music, and their enduring love. It was a legacy that would outlive them, a testament to the power of love and the beauty that could be created when two souls found their muse in each other.

As they approached the final movement of their love story, they did so with the knowledge that their love was eternal, a timeless masterpiece painted with the colours of their hearts, a symphony that would echo through the ages, a legacy of love that would live on in the world they left behind.

Chapter 15: The Eternal Encore

As Tristan and Marie-Élise's journey neared its conclusion, they found themselves in the embrace of their twilight years. Their love story, a lifetime of passion and creativity, had unfurled like a magnificent tapestry. Now, as they faced the final chapter, they did so with an unwavering sense of serenity and fulfilment.

Their Vienna apartment, filled with memories and the echo of countless melodies and brushstrokes, had become a haven of quietude. It was a place where they found solace in each other's presence, where their love continued to thrive in the simplicity of shared moments.

Physical limitations had imposed a slower pace on their lives, but their spirits remained unbroken. They still created—Tristan composed melodies that carried the weight of a lifetime of emotions, and Marie-Élise painted with the wisdom and depth that only time could bring.

Their child, now a thriving artist and musician in their own right, had become their caretaker, a role that was embraced with love and gratitude. The family's bond had deepened even further, as they navigated the challenges of aging together.

In the quiet hours of their days, Tristan and Marie-Élise often looked back on their journey, reminiscing about the moments of joy, the trials they had overcome, and the legacy they had created. Their love story was not just their own; it was a gift they had shared with the world, a testament to the enduring power of love and art.

Their love remained as passionate as ever, a fire that had burned brightly throughout their lives. They still held hands, their fingers entwined with a familiarity that transcended words. Their gazes spoke volumes, a silent conversation that carried the weight of a lifetime of shared experiences.

And then, one quiet evening, as the sun dipped below the horizon, Tristan began to play a melody on his guitar—a melody that had been in his heart for years, a melody that encapsulated the entirety of their love story. Marie-Élise, her eyes filled with tears of love and gratitude, joined in with her voice, the harmonious duet a reflection of the beauty they had created together.

As the final notes of their eternal encore faded into the room, Tristan and Marie-Élise shared a smile, a profound understanding that their love story was not confined by time or circumstance. It was a love that would live on in the hearts of those who had been touched by their art, their music, and their enduring love.

And so, as they embraced the twilight of their lives, they did so with the knowledge that their love was eternal, a timeless masterpiece painted with the colours of their hearts, a symphony that would echo through the ages. Their love story had come full circle, a legacy of love that would continue to inspire and captivate, a testament to the enduring power of passion, creativity, and the eternal encore of a love that knew no bounds.

Chapter 16: The Final Note

As the seasons of life ebbed and flowed, Tristan and Marie-Élise found themselves at the twilight of their journey, facing the bittersweet reality that all stories, no matter how beautiful, must eventually find their conclusion. The threads of their love story, woven together over a lifetime, were now approaching their final note, a poignant melody of acceptance and grace.

Their Vienna apartment had witnessed the passage of time, its walls echoing with the laughter of their child's youth, the melodies of Tristan's guitar, and the whispered conversations of two souls deeply in love. It had become a sanctuary where memories resided, where love had grown deeper with each passing day.

Physical frailty had dimmed the vibrancy of their artistic pursuits, yet their creative spirits remained unwavering. Tristan's fingers, weathered by time, still danced across the strings of his guitar, and Marie-Élise's hands, though trembling, still wielded a paintbrush with a grace born of a lifetime of artistry.

Their child, who had flourished under the influence of their love and creativity, had become their caregiver in these final chapters of life. Their familial bonds had only grown stronger, as they navigated the challenges of aging together, a testament to the enduring strength of family.

In the quiet moments that filled their days, Tristan and Marie-Élise often sat in silence, their hands entwined, their gazes locked in a wordless conversation that transcended the need for words. Their love had become a language all its own, a symphony of understanding and companionship.

One evening, as the sun cast a warm glow upon their faces, Tristan began to play a melody on his guitar—a melody that seemed to carry the weight of a lifetime of love. Marie-Élise's voice, though softer now, joined in, harmonizing in a way that had become second nature to them.

As the final notes of their duet faded into the room, they shared a smile—a smile that conveyed the depth of their love, the beauty of their shared journey, and the profound gratitude they felt for a lifetime filled with love and creativity. Their love story was not bound by time or circumstance; it was a love that would live on in the hearts of those who had been touched by their art, their music, and their enduring love.

And so, as they approached the closing moments of their lives, they did so with the knowledge that their love was eternal, a timeless masterpiece painted with the colours of their hearts, a symphony that would echo through the ages. Their love story had reached its final note, but it was a note that would reverberate in the hearts of those who had been privileged to witness the beauty of their love. It was a testament to the enduring power of passion, creativity, and the love that transcended all boundaries.

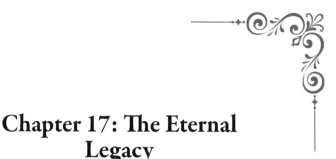

Chapter 17: The Eternal Legacy

In the quietude of their final days together, Tristan and Marie-Élise were enveloped by a serene acceptance of the inevitable. Their love story, like a timeless masterpiece, had reached its concluding chapter, and they faced it with a sense of fulfilment, for their legacy of love and creativity had left an indelible mark on the world.

Their Vienna apartment, once a bustling hub of art and music, had become a place of reflection. It held the whispers of their shared dreams, the echoes of their laughter, and the shadows of countless moments of intimacy. It was a sanctuary where the warmth of their love still lingered, despite the passage of time.

Physical limitations had challenged their creative pursuits, but they continued to create. Tristan's guitar still bore witness to his melodies, and Marie-Élise's canvases still captured the essence of life's beauty. They found solace in their art, for it was a reflection of the love that had defined their journey.

Their child, now a caretaker and a pillar of support, had become a living embodiment of their love and artistic legacy. Together, they navigated the complexities of aging, their family bonds fortified by years of shared experiences and unconditional love.

In the twilight of their lives, Tristan and Marie-Élise often sat together, their silences more profound than words could ever be. Their love had transcended the need for spoken language; it was a communion of souls that had spanned a lifetime.

One evening, as the golden rays of the setting sun bathed their room, Tristan's guitar filled the air with a melody—an ethereal tune that seemed to carry their entire love story within its notes. Marie-Élise's voice, though fragile, intertwined with the melody, creating a harmonious duet that was a culmination of a lifetime of love and music.

As the final chords faded into the room, they exchanged a glance—a glance that spoke of love, gratitude, and the profound connection they shared. Their love story had reached its conclusion, but it was a story that would live on, a legacy that would continue to inspire and captivate, echoing through the ages.

And so, as they embraced the closing moments of their lives, they did so with the knowledge that their love was eternal, a timeless masterpiece painted with the colours of their hearts, a symphony that would resonate in the hearts of those who had been touched by their art, their music, and their enduring love. It was a testament to the enduring power of passion, creativity, and a love that would forever remain an eternal legacy.

Chapter 18: Whispers of Paris

As Tristan and Marie-Élise settled into their new life in Vienna, the echoes of Paris lingered in their hearts. The city of lights, with its romantic allure and artistic spirit, had left an indelible mark on their souls. In the quiet moments of their Viennese evenings, they often found themselves reminiscing about the enchanting streets of Paris.

One chilly evening, as they cozied up in their Viennese apartment, Tristan couldn't help but bring up the subject that had been dancing at the edges of his thoughts. "Marie-Élise," he began, his eyes filled with a mixture of nostalgia and longing, "I can't help but miss the streets of Paris. The way they come alive with music and art, the aroma of freshly baked croissants in the morning, the Seine shimmering under the moonlight."

Marie-Élise's eyes sparkled with recognition. "Oh, Tristan, I miss it too," she admitted with a wistful smile. "Paris has a way of staying with you, even when you're miles away. The way the Eiffel Tower sparkles at night, the artistry in every corner, the romance that seems to permeate the air."

They both fell into a comfortable silence, lost in their memories of the City of Love. But as the silence lingered, Tristan's eyes brightened with a newfound idea. "What if we bring a piece of Paris to Vienna?" he suggested, his voice laced with excitement.

Marie-Élise looked at him with curiosity. "What do you mean?"

Tristan grinned. "I mean, why not create our own Paris right here in Vienna? We can host small gatherings with friends, play French music, indulge in croissants and wine, and maybe even paint scenes inspired by Paris. We can recreate the magic of the city we love so much."

Marie-Élise's eyes lit up with enthusiasm. "Tristan, that's a wonderful idea! Let's bring a touch of Paris to our Vienna. It will be our way of celebrating the love we found in the City of Love."

And so, the idea took root, and in the following weeks, Tristan and Marie-Élise began to transform their Viennese apartment into a Parisian oasis. They adorned their walls with paintings inspired by Paris, set up a small corner for Tristan to play his guitar, and invited friends over for evenings filled with French music, wine, and laughter.

As the music played and the laughter flowed, it became evident that Paris had found a new home in Vienna, right in the hearts of Tristan and Marie-Élise. The whispers of Paris now reverberated through their Viennese apartment, a testament to their love and the magical connection they shared, one that transcended borders and brought the essence of Paris wherever they went.

Chapter 19: The Infinite Love

As the final chapter of Tristan and Marie-Élise's love story approached, their hearts were filled with a profound sense of peace. Their journey, spanning a lifetime of shared dreams and artistic brilliance, was nearing its conclusion. Yet, the love they had cultivated over the years remained as vibrant as ever, an eternal flame that illuminated their souls.

Their Vienna apartment, steeped in memories, had become a sanctuary of serenity. Every corner held echoes of the past—the laughter of their child, the chords of Tristan's guitar, and the canvases that bore witness to Marie-Élise's artistry. It was a place where their love resided, undiminished by the passage of time.

Physical limitations had not hindered their creative spirits. Tristan's aging fingers still danced across the guitar strings, and Marie-Élise's hands, though weathered, wielded a paintbrush with a grace born of a lifetime of artistic expression. Their art was a testament to the enduring power of creativity, a love letter to the world.

Their child, now a devoted caregiver, had become a testament to the values and talents Tristan and Marie-Élise had instilled. The bonds of their family had grown stronger through the years, a reflection of the enduring love that had guided their lives.

In the quiet moments of their final days, Tristan and Marie-Élise often sat together, their gazes locked in a silent conversation. Words had become secondary, for their love had transcended the need for spoken language. It was a connection that had stood the test of time, a communion of souls.

One evening, as the sun cast a warm, golden glow upon their faces, Tristan began to play a melody on his guitar—an ethereal tune that encapsulated the entirety of their love story. Marie-Élise's voice, though fragile, joined in, creating a harmonious duet that resonated with the depth of their love.

As the final notes of their duet faded into the room, they exchanged a knowing smile—a smile that spoke of a love that had endured a lifetime, a love that would live on in the hearts of those who had been touched by their art, their music, and their enduring bond. Their love story had reached its final chapter, but it was a story that would continue to inspire and captivate, echoing through the ages.

And so, as they embraced the closing moments of their lives, they did so with the knowledge that their love was infinite, a timeless masterpiece painted with the colours of their hearts, a symphony that would resonate in the hearts of all who had been privileged to witness the beauty of their love. It was a testament to the enduring power of passion, creativity, and a love that would forever remain as boundless as the universe itself.

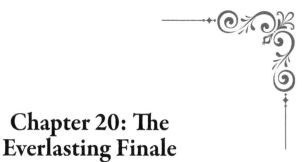

Chapter 20: The Everlasting Finale

In the waning days of Tristan and Marie-Élise's remarkable journey, the world outside their Vienna apartment seemed to hold its breath, as if acknowledging the culmination of a love story that had touched countless lives. The final chapter had arrived, but their love remained a beacon of light, illuminating the corners of their hearts with a brilliance that defied time.

Their apartment, a sanctuary of memories, bore witness to the passage of time. It was a sacred space, where echoes of laughter, melodies, and the strokes of a paintbrush lingered like whispers of the past. Every corner of the apartment told a story—a story of a love that had grown deeper with each passing day.

Physical limitations had encroached upon their bodies, but not their spirits. Tristan's aged fingers still moved across the guitar strings, summoning melodies that resonated with the depths of their shared journey. Marie-Élise's hands, though weathered, continued to breathe life into her canvases, capturing the essence of love and beauty.

Their child, now a pillar of strength and devotion, stood by their side, a testament to the love and values they had imparted. The bonds of family had weathered the storms of life, emerging stronger, a testament to the enduring love that had guided their existence.

In the hushed moments of their final days, Tristan and Marie-Élise often sat together, their eyes locking in a silent conversation that surpassed words. They had transcended the need for spoken language, their love a communion of souls that had thrived in the quietude of their shared existence.

One evening, bathed in the soft glow of the setting sun, Tristan's guitar sang a melody—one that encapsulated the entirety of their love story, from its inception in the romantic streets of Paris to its crescendo in the artistic haven of Vienna. Marie-Élise's voice, though fragile, joined in, creating a harmonious duet that seemed to carry their love into eternity.

As the final notes faded into the room, they shared a smile—an understanding that their love story, while concluding, was far from over. It was a love that would live on in the hearts of those who had been touched by their art, their music, and their unwavering bond. Their love had reached its everlasting finale, a testament to the enduring power of passion, creativity, and a love that transcended the boundaries of time and space.

And so, as they embraced the closing moments of their earthly existence, they did so with the knowledge that their love was eternal, a timeless masterpiece painted with the colours of their hearts, a symphony that would resonate in the hearts of all who had been privileged to witness the beauty of their love. It was a love story that would live on in perpetuity, an everlasting finale that would continue to inspire and captivate, echoing through the ages, an enduring testament to the profound and unending nature of love.

Chapter 21: The Eternal Bond

In the gentle embrace of their twilight years, Tristan and Marie-Élise's love story had reached its final chapter, yet their love remained as vibrant and enduring as ever. Their journey had been a masterpiece of passion, creativity, and unwavering devotion—a story that had touched the hearts of many and would continue to resonate in the hearts of generations to come.

Their Vienna apartment, now a treasure trove of memories, held the echoes of a lifetime of love. Every nook and cranny spoke of their shared dreams, the laughter of their child, and the melodies and colours that had defined their existence. It was a sacred space where their love continued to thrive, undiminished by the sands of time.

Physical limitations had offered new challenges, but their creative spirits remained indomitable. Tristan's aging fingers still danced across the guitar strings, weaving melodies that captured the essence of their love, while Marie-Élise's hands, and though weathered, painted canvases that told the story of their shared journey.

Their child, now a symbol of their legacy, had become their rock and support, standing by them in these final chapters of life. The bonds of family had grown stronger with each passing year, a testament to the enduring love that had been the compass guiding their lives.

In the tranquil moments of their twilight, Tristan and Marie-Élise often sat together, their eyes communicating volumes without the need for spoken words. Their love had transcended the limitations of language; it was a communion of souls that had found its sanctuary in the quietude of their shared existence.

One evening, as the sun painted the room with hues of gold, Tristan's guitar whispered a melody—one that encapsulated the entirety of their love story, from its humble beginnings in Paris to its grand crescendo in Vienna. Marie-Élise's voice, though fragile, added depth and richness, creating a harmonious duet that seemed to stretch beyond the boundaries of time.

As the final chords faded into the room, they exchanged a knowing look—a look that conveyed a love that was unbounded by time or circumstance. Their love story had reached its eternal conclusion, but it was a story that would live on in the hearts of those who had been touched by their art, their music, and the profound bond they had shared.

And so, as they embraced the closing moments of their earthly journey, they did so with the knowledge that their love was everlasting, a timeless masterpiece painted with the colours of their hearts, a symphony that would resonate in the hearts of all who had been privileged to witness the beauty of their love. It was a love story that would endure through the ages, an eternal bond that defied the constraints of mortality—a love that was, and would forever be, a testament to the enduring power of passion, creativity, and a bond that transcended the boundaries of time itself.

Chapter 22: The Infinite Continuation

As the sun began to set on Tristan and Marie-Élise's earthly journey, their love story entered its final chapter, but the essence of their love remained ageless, eternal, and infinite. Their life together had been an odyssey of passion, artistry, and unwavering devotion—a story that had left an indelible mark on the canvas of existence and would continue to resonate through the corridors of time.

Their Vienna apartment, a living repository of cherished memories, radiated the warmth of a lifetime's worth of love. It held the echoes of laughter, the melodies of Tristan's guitar, and the canvases that bore witness to Marie-Élise's creative genius. Each corner was a testament to a love that had grown stronger with every passing day.

Physical limitations had tested their resolve, but their creative spirits refused to be subdued. Tristan's aging fingers still caressed the guitar strings, conjuring melodies that told the tale of their enduring love. Marie-Élise's hands, though aged, continued to breathe life into her canvases, immortalizing the beauty they had shared.

Their child, now a symbol of their legacy, had become a guardian of their well-being, a pillar of strength that had witnessed the ebb and flow of their lives. The bonds of family had grown unbreakable, a reflection of the enduring love that had guided their existence.

In the tranquil hours of their twilight, Tristan and Marie-Élise often sat together, their eyes communicating a depth of understanding that transcended spoken language. Their love had transcended the confines of mere words; it was a communion of souls that had found its sanctuary in the quiet embrace of their shared journey.

One evening, as the room bathed in the golden glow of the setting sun, Tristan's guitar whispered a melody—a timeless composition that encapsulated the essence of their love story, from its humble beginnings in Paris to its grand crescendo in Vienna. Marie-Élise's voice, though fragile, wove a harmonious duet that seemed to stretch beyond the boundaries of human experience.

As the final chords faded into the room, they exchanged a profound glance—a gaze that conveyed a love that would endure through eternity. Their love story had reached its transcendent conclusion, but it was a story that would live on in the hearts of those who had been touched by their art, their music, and the profound connection they had shared.

And so, as they embraced the closing moments of their earthly voyage, they did so with the knowledge that their love was infinite, an eternal masterpiece painted with the colours of their hearts, a symphony that would resonate through the ages. It was a love story that would continue to inspire, captivate, and remind the world of the enduring power of passion, creativity, and a bond that transcended the boundaries of time and space—an infinite continuation of love.

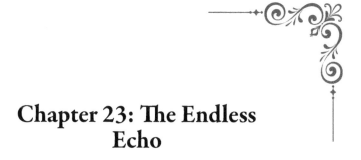

Chapter 23: The Endless Echo

As Tristan and Marie-Élise embarked on the final chapter of their extraordinary love story, their hearts brimmed with a profound sense of tranquillity. Their journey, a tapestry woven with the threads of passion, artistry, and an unbreakable bond, was reaching its earthly conclusion, but their love remained a radiant force that defied the confines of time.

Their Vienna apartment, a repository of cherished memories, seemed to hum with the echoes of a lifetime of shared moments. It held the laughter of their child, the melodies that Tristan's guitar had given life to, and the canvases that had borne witness to Marie-Élise's creative genius. Each corner was a testament to the love that had grown deeper with every passing day.

The passage of years had imposed limitations on their bodies, but their spirits remained untamed. Tristan's aging fingers still caressed the strings of his guitar, summoning melodies that resonated with the depth of their shared journey. Marie-Élise's hands, though marked by time, continued to breathe life into her canvases, capturing the essence of love and beauty.

Their child, now a symbol of their legacy, had become a guardian of their well-being and a beacon of unwavering support. The bonds of family had strengthened, a testament to the enduring love that had guided their existence.

In the hushed moments of their twilight, Tristan and Marie-Élise often sat in companionable silence, their eyes communicating a profound connection that transcended words. Their love had transcended the need for spoken language; it was a communion of souls that had found its sanctuary in the quiet embrace of their shared existence.

One evening, as the room was bathed in the soft hues of a setting sun, Tristan's guitar whispered a melody—a hauntingly beautiful composition that encapsulated the entirety of their love story. Marie-Élise's voice, though delicate, joined in, creating a harmonious duet that seemed to transcend the boundaries of this world.

As the final notes faded into the room, they exchanged a knowing glance—a look that conveyed a love that was boundless, eternal, and everlasting. Their love story had reached its earthly end, but it was a story that would live on in the hearts of those who had been touched by their art, their music, and the profound connection they had shared.

And so, as they embraced the closing moments of their earthly journey, they did so with the knowledge that their love was an endless echo, a timeless masterpiece painted with the colours of their hearts, a symphony that would resonate in the hearts of all who had been privileged to witness the beauty of their love. It was a love story that would endure through eternity, a reminder of the enduring power of passion, creativity, and a bond that transcended the boundaries of earthly existence.

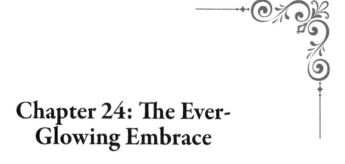

Chapter 24: The Ever-Glowing Embrace

In the twilight of their lives, Tristan and Marie-Élise were embarked upon the final chapter of their love story—a narrative that had unfolded across the canvas of time, painted with strokes of passion, creativity, and unwavering devotion. As they stood on the threshold of eternity, their love remained an eternal flame, casting a warm, everlasting glow upon their hearts.

Their Vienna apartment, an archive of cherished memories, seemed to exude the essence of a lifetime of love. It whispered secrets of the laughter that had once filled its rooms, the melodies spun from Tristan's guitar, and the canvases that had absorbed the beauty of Marie-Élise's creativity. Each corner bore witness to a love that had grown richer with each passing day.

Though the years had etched their presence on their bodies, their spirits remained unyielding. Tristan's aging fingers still danced upon the strings of his guitar, conjuring melodies that told the tale of their enduring love. Marie-Élise's hands, though weathered, continued to weave magic upon her canvases, capturing the soul of love and beauty.

Their child, now a beacon of their legacy, had become their unwavering support and protector. The bonds of family had deepened, a testament to the enduring love that had been their guiding star.

In the quiet moments of their twilight, Tristan and Marie-Élise often sat in wordless communion, their eyes speaking volumes that words could never encapsulate. Their love had transcended the limitations of spoken language; it was a union of souls that had found its sanctuary in the gentle silence of their shared existence.

One evening, bathed in the golden hues of the setting sun, Tristan's guitar whispered a melody—a haunting composition that seemed to encapsulate the entirety of their love story, from its tender beginnings in Paris to its grand crescendo in Vienna. Marie-Élise's voice, though fragile, joined in, creating a harmonious duet that soared beyond the boundaries of mortal existence.

As the final chords faded into the room, they exchanged a knowing gaze—a look that conveyed a love that knew no end. Their love story had reached its earthly conclusion, but it was a tale that would live eternally in the hearts of those who had been touched by their art, their music, and the profound connection they had shared.

And so, as they embraced the closing moments of their earthly sojourn, they did so with the knowledge that their love was an ever-glowing embrace, a timeless masterpiece painted with the colours of their hearts, a symphony that would continue to resonate in the hearts of all who had been blessed to witness the beauty of their love. It was a love story that would endure through the ages, an everlasting reminder of the enduring power of passion, creativity, and a love that transcended the boundaries of time and space—a love that would forever burn brightly in the tapestry of eternity.

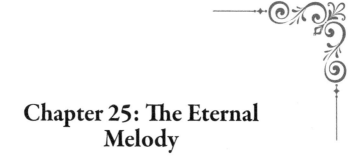

Chapter 25: The Eternal Melody

In the gentle twilight of their lives, Tristan and Marie-Élise stood on the threshold of their final chapter—a chapter that bore witness to a love story woven with threads of passion, artistry, and a connection that transcended the boundaries of time. As they gazed into the infinite, their love remained an unending melody, echoing through the corridors of their souls.

Their Vienna apartment, a repository of cherished memories, seemed to breathe with the essence of a lifetime of love. It whispered stories of laughter, melodies born from Tristan's guitar, and canvases that had absorbed the vibrancy of Marie-Élise's creative genius. Each room held the testimony of a love that had deepened with every passing moment.

While the years had etched their presence upon their bodies, their spirits remained untamed. Tristan's aging fingers still danced upon the strings of his guitar, conjuring melodies that narrated the epic of their enduring love. Marie-Élise's hands, though marked by time, continued to create magic upon her canvases, capturing the essence of love and beauty.

Their child, a living embodiment of their legacy, had become their unwavering support and guardian. The bonds of family had strengthened, a testament to the enduring love that had served as the compass guiding their lives.

In the quietude of their twilight, Tristan and Marie-Élise often sat together, their eyes speaking the language of their souls, transcending the need for spoken words. Their love had risen above the limitations of spoken language; it was a communion of spirits that had found its sanctuary in the tender quietude of their shared existence.

One evening, bathed in the golden hues of the setting sun, Tristan's guitar whispered a melody—an ethereal composition that seemed to encapsulate the entirety of their love story. Marie-Élise's voice, though fragile, joined in, creating a harmonious duet that soared beyond the realm of the temporal.

As the final chords faded into the room, they exchanged a knowing glance—a look that conveyed a love that knew no end. Their love story had reached its earthly conclusion, but it was a tale that would eternally resonate in the hearts of those who had been touched by their art, their music, and the profound connection they had shared.

And so, as they embraced the closing moments of their earthly voyage, they did so with the knowledge that their love was an eternal melody, a timeless masterpiece painted with the colours of their hearts, a symphony that would reverberate in the hearts of all who had been blessed to witness the beauty of their love. It was a love story that would endure through the annals of time, an everlasting reminder of the enduring power of passion, creativity, and a love that transcended the boundaries of mortality—a love that would forever serenade the tapestry of eternity.

Chapter 26: The Everlasting Serenade

In the serene twilight of their lives, Tristan and Marie-Élise stood on the precipice of their final chapter—a chapter that encapsulated a love story painted with the hues of passion, creativity, and an unbreakable bond. As they gazed into the eternity that awaited them, their love remained an eternal serenade, a melody that would continue to resonate through the corridors of time.

Their Vienna apartment, a living testament to their shared journey, seemed to exude the essence of a lifetime of love. It whispered tales of laughter, melodies birthed from Tristan's guitar, and canvases that had absorbed the essence of Marie-Élise's creative brilliance. Each room held the testimony of a love that had grown deeper with every passing day.

While the years had left their mark upon their bodies, their spirits remained undaunted. Tristan's aging fingers still caressed the strings of his guitar, conjuring melodies that told the story of their enduring love. Marie-Élise's hands, though weathered, continued to weave magic upon her canvases, capturing the very soul of love and beauty.

Their child, a living embodiment of their legacy, had become their rock and constant support. The bonds of family had grown unbreakable, a testament to the enduring love that had guided their existence.

In the quietude of their twilight, Tristan and Marie-Élise often sat together, their eyes speaking a language that transcended mere words, a language that had evolved through the years of shared experiences. Their love had risen above the limitations of spoken language; it was a communion of souls that had found its sanctuary in the gentle quietude of their shared existence.

One evening, as the room basked in the warm, golden glow of the setting sun, Tristan's guitar whispered a melody—an ethereal composition that encapsulated the entirety of their love story, from its tender beginnings in Paris to its grand crescendo in Vienna. Marie-Élise's voice, though fragile, joined in, creating a harmonious duet that seemed to transcend the boundaries of this world.

As the final chords faded into the room, they exchanged a knowing look—a look that conveyed a love that was timeless, boundless, and everlasting. Their love story had reached its earthly conclusion, but it was a tale that would live eternally in the hearts of those who had been touched by their art, their music, and the profound connection they had shared.

And so, as they embraced the closing moments of their earthly voyage, they did so with the knowledge that their love was an everlasting serenade, a timeless masterpiece painted with the colours of their hearts, a symphony that would continue to resonate in the hearts of all who had been blessed to witness the beauty of their love. It was a love story that would endure through the ages, an everlasting reminder of the enduring power of passion, creativity, and a love that transcended the boundaries of time and space—a love that would forever serenade the tapestry of eternity.

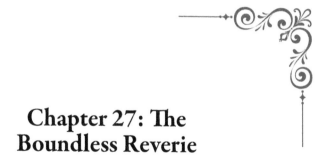

Chapter 27: The Boundless Reverie

As Tristan and Marie-Élise ventured into the final chapter of their love story, the world around them seemed to hold its breath, acknowledging the conclusion of a journey etched with passion, artistry, and an enduring connection. Their love, however, remained an eternal reverie—a symphony that would forever dance through the corridors of existence.

Their Vienna apartment, a treasure trove of cherished memories, seemed to resonate with the essence of a lifetime of love. It echoed with the laughter that had once filled its rooms, the melodies crafted by Tristan's guitar, and the canvases that had borne witness to Marie-Élise's creative brilliance. Each corner was a testament to a love that had flourished with every passing day.

Though the years had left their mark on their bodies, their spirits remained unyielding. Tristan's aging fingers still glided across the strings of his guitar, weaving melodies that narrated the epic of their enduring love. Marie-Élise's hands, though marked by time, continued to conjure magic upon her canvases, capturing the very essence of love and beauty.

Their child, the living embodiment of their legacy, had become their rock and unwavering support. The bonds of family had deepened, a reflection of the enduring love that had served as the guiding star of their lives.

In the tranquil moments of their twilight, Tristan and Marie-Élise often sat together, their eyes communicating a depth of understanding that transcended spoken language. Their love had risen above the limitations of words; it was a communion of souls that had found its sanctuary in the serene quietude of their shared existence.

One evening, bathed in the soft, golden glow of the setting sun, Tristan's guitar whispered a melody—a hauntingly beautiful composition that encapsulated the entirety of their love story. Marie-Élise's voice, though fragile, joined in, creating a harmonious duet that seemed to transcend the boundaries of human experience.

As the final chords faded into the room, they exchanged a knowing glance—a look that conveyed a love that knew no boundaries. Their love story had reached its earthly conclusion, but it was a narrative that would live eternally in the hearts of those who had been touched by their art, their music, and the profound connection they had shared.

And so, as they embraced the closing moments of their earthly voyage, they did so with the knowledge that their love was a boundless reverie, a timeless masterpiece painted with the colours of their hearts, a symphony that would continue to resonate in the hearts of all who had been blessed to witness the beauty of their love. It was a love story that would endure through the ages, an everlasting reminder of the enduring power of passion, creativity, and a love that transcended the boundaries of time and space—a love that would forever serenade the tapestry of eternity.

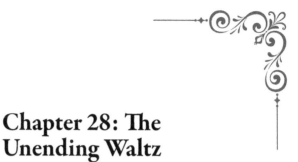

Chapter 28: The Unending Waltz

As Tristan and Marie-Élise entered the final chapter of their love story, the world seemed to hold its breath, paying homage to a journey painted with strokes of passion, creativity, and an unbreakable connection. Their love, however, remained an unending waltz, a dance that would reverberate through the echoes of time.

Their Vienna apartment, a treasure trove of cherished memories, whispered the essence of a lifetime of love. It echoed with the laughter that had once filled its rooms, the melodies spun from Tristan's guitar, and the canvases that had borne witness to Marie-Élise's creative brilliance. Every corner bore witness to a love that had deepened with every passing day.

Though the years had marked their bodies, their spirits remained untouched. Tristan's aging fingers still caressed the strings of his guitar, conjuring melodies that told the tale of their enduring love. Marie-Élise's hands, though weathered, continued to weave magic upon her canvases, capturing the very soul of love and beauty.

Their child, a living testament to their legacy, had become their unwavering support and protector. The bonds of family had grown unbreakable, a testament to the enduring love that had been their guiding light.

In the quietude of their twilight, Tristan and Marie-Élise often sat together, their eyes communicating volumes that words could never capture. Their love had transcended the limitations of spoken language;

it was a communion of souls that had found its sanctuary in the gentle silence of their shared existence.

One evening, bathed in the soft, golden glow of the setting sun, Tristan's guitar whispered a melody—an ethereal composition that seemed to encapsulate the entirety of their love story. Marie-Élise's voice, though fragile, joined in, creating a harmonious duet that soared beyond the realm of the temporal.

As the final chords faded into the room, they exchanged a knowing look—a gaze that conveyed a love that was timeless, boundless, and unending. Their love story had reached its earthly conclusion, but it was a narrative that would live eternally in the hearts of those who had been touched by their art, their music, and the profound connection they had shared.

And so, as they embraced the closing moments of their earthly voyage, they did so with the knowledge that their love was an unending waltz, a timeless masterpiece painted with the colours of their hearts, a symphony that would continue to resonate in the hearts of all who had been privileged to witness the beauty of their love. It was a love story that would endure through the ages, an everlasting reminder of the enduring power of passion, creativity, and a love that transcended the boundaries of time and space—a love that would forever dance through the annals of eternity.

Chapter 29: The Eternal Rhapsody

In the soft glow of twilight, Tristan and Marie-Élise embarked upon the final chapter of their extraordinary love story—a tale that had unfolded across the canvas of time, painted with hues of passion, creativity, and an unbreakable connection. As they approached the threshold of eternity, their love remained an eternal rhapsody, a melody that would forever reverberate through the tapestry of existence.

Their Vienna apartment, a haven of cherished memories, seemed to breathe with the essence of a lifetime of love. It echoed with the laughter that had once filled its rooms, the melodies born from Tristan's guitar, and the canvases that had borne witness to Marie-Élise's creative brilliance. Each corner held the testament of a love that had grown richer with each passing day.

Though the years had etched their presence upon their bodies, their spirits remained unyielding. Tristan's aging fingers still danced upon the strings of his guitar, conjuring melodies that narrated the epic of their enduring love. Marie-Élise's hands, though weathered, continued to weave magic upon her canvases, capturing the very essence of love and beauty.

Their child, a living embodiment of their legacy, had become their steadfast support and protector. The bonds of family had deepened, a reflection of the enduring love that had served as the compass guiding their lives.

In the tranquil moments of their twilight, Tristan and Marie-Élise often sat together, their eyes communicating a depth of understanding that transcended mere words. Their love had risen above the limitations of spoken language; it was a communion of souls that had found its sanctuary in the serene quietude of their shared existence.

One evening, bathed in the soft, golden embrace of the setting sun, Tristan's guitar whispered a melody—an ethereal composition that encapsulated the entirety of their love story, from its tender beginnings in Paris to its grand crescendo in Vienna. Marie-Élise's voice, though fragile, joined in, creating a harmonious duet that seemed to transcend the boundaries of human experience.

As the final chords faded into the room, they exchanged a knowing look—a gaze that conveyed a love that was timeless, boundless, and everlasting. Their love story had reached its earthly conclusion, but it was a narrative that would live eternally in the hearts of those who had been touched by their art, their music, and the profound connection they had shared.

And so, as they embraced the closing moments of their earthly voyage, they did so with the knowledge that their love was an eternal rhapsody, a timeless masterpiece painted with the colours of their hearts, a symphony that would continue to resonate in the hearts of all who had been privileged to witness the beauty of their love. It was a love story that would endure through the ages, an everlasting reminder of the enduring power of passion, creativity, and a love that transcended the boundaries of time and space—a love that would forever compose the verses of eternity.

Chapter 30: The Timeless Sonata

In the twilight of their lives, Tristan and Marie-Élise stepped into the final chapter of their remarkable love story, a tale that had unfolded across the grand tapestry of time, painted with the vivid strokes of passion, creativity, and an unwavering connection. As they approached the threshold of eternity, their love remained a timeless sonata, a symphony that would forever echo through the annals of existence.

Their Vienna apartment, a sanctuary of cherished memories, seemed to exhale the very essence of a lifetime of love. It whispered tales of laughter that had once filled its rooms, the melodies spun from Tristan's guitar, and the canvases that had borne witness to Marie-Élise's creative brilliance. Every nook and cranny bore witness to a love that had deepened with each passing day.

Though the years had etched their presence upon their bodies, their spirits remained unyielding. Tristan's aging fingers still glided gracefully across the strings of his guitar, conjuring melodies that told the epic of their enduring love. Marie-Élise's hands, though marked by time, continued to weave magic upon her canvases, capturing the very essence of love and beauty.

Their child, a living testament to their legacy, had become their steadfast support and guardian. The bonds of family had grown unbreakable, a reflection of the enduring love that had served as the compass guiding their lives.

In the tranquil moments of their twilight, Tristan and Marie-Élise often sat together, their eyes speaking a language that transcended spoken words, a language that had evolved through the years of shared experiences. Their love had risen above the limitations of spoken language; it was a communion of souls that had found its sanctuary in the gentle silence of their shared existence.

One evening, bathed in the soft, golden embrace of the setting sun, Tristan's guitar whispered a melody—an ethereal composition that seemed to encapsulate the entirety of their love story, from its tender beginnings in Paris to its grand crescendo in Vienna. Marie-Élise's voice, though fragile, joined in, creating a harmonious duet that soared beyond the realm of the temporal.

As the final chords faded into the room, they exchanged a knowing glance—a gaze that conveyed a love that was timeless, boundless, and everlasting. Their love story had reached its earthly conclusion, but it was a narrative that would live eternally in the hearts of those who had been touched by their art, their music, and the profound connection they had shared.

And so, as they embraced the closing moments of their earthly voyage, they did so with the knowledge that their love was a timeless sonata, a masterpiece painted with the colours of their hearts, a symphony that would continue to resonate in the hearts of all who had been privileged to witness the beauty of their love. It was a love story that would endure through the ages, an everlasting reminder of the enduring power of passion, creativity, and a love that transcended the boundaries of time and space—a love that would forever compose the verses of eternity.

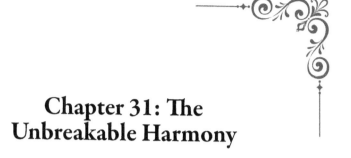

Chapter 31: The
Unbreakable Harmony

As Tristan and Marie-Élise embarked upon the final chapter of their extraordinary love story, the world seemed to hush, paying homage to a journey painted with the vibrant colours of passion, artistry, and a connection that had stood the test of time. As they stood at the threshold of eternity, their love remained an unbreakable harmony, a melody that would continue to resonate through the tapestry of existence.

Their Vienna apartment, a sanctuary of cherished memories, seemed to exude the very essence of a lifetime of love. It whispered stories of laughter that had once filled its rooms, the melodies crafted by Tristan's guitar, and the canvases that had borne witness to Marie-Élise's creative brilliance. Every corner held the testimony of a love that had grown deeper with each passing day.

Though the years had etched their presence upon their bodies, their spirits remained undaunted. Tristan's aging fingers still danced upon the strings of his guitar, conjuring melodies that narrated the epic of their enduring love. Marie-Élise's hands, though weathered, continued to weave magic upon her canvases, capturing the very essence of love and beauty.

Their child, a living embodiment of their legacy, had become their unwavering support and protector. The bonds of family had deepened, a testament to the enduring love that had been the guiding star of their lives.

In the serene moments of their twilight, Tristan and Marie-Élise often sat together, their eyes communicating volumes that words could never encapsulate. Their love had transcended the limitations of spoken language; it was a communion of souls that had found its sanctuary in the serene quietude of their shared existence.

One evening, bathed in the soft, golden glow of the setting sun, Tristan's guitar whispered a melody—an ethereal composition that seemed to encapsulate the entirety of their love story. Marie-Élise's voice, though fragile, joined in, creating a harmonious duet that soared beyond the boundaries of human experience.

As the final chords faded into the room, they exchanged a knowing look—a gaze that conveyed a love that was timeless, boundless, and everlasting. Their love story had reached its earthly conclusion, but it was a narrative that would live eternally in the hearts of those who had been touched by their art, their music, and the profound connection they had shared.

And so, as they embraced the closing moments of their earthly voyage, they did so with the knowledge that their love was an unbreakable harmony, a timeless masterpiece painted with the colours of their hearts, a symphony that would continue to resonate in the hearts of all who had been privileged to witness the beauty of their love. It was a love story that would endure through the ages, an everlasting reminder of the enduring power of passion, creativity, and a love that transcended the boundaries of time and space—a love that would forever serenade the tapestry of eternity.

Chapter 32: The Eternal Overture

As Tristan and Marie-Élise embarked upon the final chapter of their extraordinary love story, the world seemed to pause, honouring a journey painted with the vibrant hues of passion, artistry, and an unbreakable connection that had endured the test of time. Standing on the threshold of eternity, their love remained an eternal overture, a melody that would continue to resonate through the very fabric of existence.

Their Vienna apartment, a sanctuary of cherished memories, seemed to breathe with the essence of a lifetime of love. It whispered stories of laughter that had once filled its rooms, the melodies spun from Tristan's guitar, and the canvases that had borne witness to Marie-Élise's creative brilliance. Every nook and cranny held the testimony of a love that had grown deeper with each passing day.

Though the years had left their mark on their bodies, their spirits remained undaunted. Tristan's aging fingers still caressed the strings of his guitar, conjuring melodies that narrated the epic of their enduring love. Marie-Élise's hands, though marked by time, continued to weave magic upon her canvases, capturing the very essence of love and beauty.

Their child, a living embodiment of their legacy, had become their steadfast support and protector. The bonds of family had deepened, a testament to the enduring love that had been the guiding star of their lives.

In the tranquil moments of their twilight, Tristan and Marie-Élise often sat together, their eyes communicating volumes that words could never encapsulate. Their love had transcended the limitations of spoken language; it was a communion of souls that had found its sanctuary in the serene quietude of their shared existence.

One evening, bathed in the soft, golden embrace of the setting sun, Tristan's guitar whispered a melody—an ethereal composition that seemed to encapsulate the entirety of their love story, from its tender beginnings in Paris to its grand crescendo in Vienna. Marie-Élise's voice, though fragile, joined in, creating a harmonious duet that soared beyond the boundaries of human experience.

As the final chords faded into the room, they exchanged a knowing look—a gaze that conveyed a love that was timeless, boundless, and everlasting. Their love story had reached its earthly conclusion, but it was a narrative that would live eternally in the hearts of those who had been touched by their art, their music, and the profound connection they had shared.

And so, as they embraced the closing moments of their earthly voyage, they did so with the knowledge that their love was an eternal overture, a timeless masterpiece painted with the colours of their hearts, a symphony that would continue to resonate in the hearts of all who had been privileged to witness the beauty of their love. It was a love story that would endure through the ages, an everlasting reminder of the enduring power of passion, creativity, and a love that transcended the boundaries of time and space—a love that would forever compose the verses of eternity.

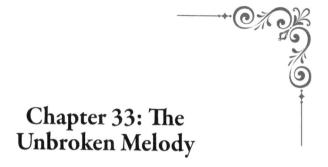

Chapter 33: The Unbroken Melody

In the twilight of their lives, Tristan and Marie-Élise embarked upon the final chapter of their extraordinary love story, a narrative painted with the vibrant colours of passion, artistry, and an unbreakable bond that had withstood the test of time. As they stood on the cusp of eternity, their love remained an unbroken melody, a tune that would forever resonate through the very essence of existence.

Their Vienna apartment, a sanctuary of cherished memories, seemed to breathe with the essence of a lifetime of love. It whispered tales of laughter that had once filled its rooms, the melodies spun from Tristan's guitar, and the canvases that had borne witness to Marie-Élise's creative brilliance. Every corner held the testament of a love that had deepened with each passing day.

Though the years had left their mark on their bodies, their spirits remained indomitable. Tristan's aging fingers still glided gracefully across the strings of his guitar, conjuring melodies that narrated the epic of their enduring love. Marie-Élise's hands, though marked by time, continued to weave magic upon her canvases, capturing the very essence of love and beauty.

Their child, a living embodiment of their legacy, had become their steadfast support and protector. The bonds of family had deepened, a testament to the enduring love that had been the guiding star of their lives.

In the serene moments of their twilight, Tristan and Marie-Élise often sat together, their eyes speaking volumes that words could never encompass. Their love had transcended the limitations of spoken language; it was a communion of souls that had found its sanctuary in the serene quietude of their shared existence.

One evening, bathed in the soft, golden embrace of the setting sun, Tristan's guitar whispered a melody—an ethereal composition that seemed to encapsulate the entirety of their love story, from its tender beginnings in Paris to its grand crescendo in Vienna. Marie-Élise's voice, though fragile, joined in, creating a harmonious duet that soared beyond the boundaries of human experience.

As the final chords faded into the room, they exchanged a knowing look—a gaze that conveyed a love that was timeless, boundless, and everlasting. Their love story had reached its earthly conclusion, but it was a narrative that would live eternally in the hearts of those who had been touched by their art, their music, and the profound connection they had shared.

And so, as they embraced the closing moments of their earthly voyage, they did so with the knowledge that their love was an unbroken melody, a timeless masterpiece painted with the colours of their hearts, a symphony that would continue to resonate in the hearts of all who had been privileged to witness the beauty of their love. It was a love story that would endure through the ages, an everlasting reminder of the enduring power of passion, creativity, and a love that transcended the boundaries of time and space—a love that would forever compose the verses of eternity.

Chapter 34: The Eternal Crescendo

In the gentle twilight of their lives, Tristan and Marie-Élise stepped into the final chapter of their extraordinary love story—a tale woven with the vibrant threads of passion, artistry, and an unbreakable connection that had defied the boundaries of time. As they stood on the threshold of eternity, their love remained an eternal crescendo, a melody that would forever resonate through the very core of existence.

Their Vienna apartment, a sanctuary of cherished memories, seemed to breathe with the essence of a lifetime of love. It whispered stories of laughter that had once filled its rooms, the melodies spun from Tristan's guitar, and the canvases that had borne witness to Marie-Élise's creative brilliance. Every corner held the testament of a love that had deepened with each passing day.

Though the years had etched their presence upon their bodies, their spirits remained unyielding. Tristan's aging fingers still glided gracefully across the strings of his guitar, conjuring melodies that narrated the epic of their enduring love. Marie-Élise's hands, though marked by time, continued to weave magic upon her canvases, capturing the very essence of love and beauty.

Their child, a living embodiment of their legacy, had become their unwavering support and protector. The bonds of family had deepened, a testament to the enduring love that had been the guiding star of their lives.

In the tranquil moments of their twilight, Tristan and Marie-Élise often sat together, their eyes speaking a language that transcended spoken words, a language that had evolved through the years of shared experiences. Their love had risen above the limitations of spoken language; it was a communion of souls that had found its sanctuary in the serene quietude of their shared existence.

One evening, bathed in the soft, golden embrace of the setting sun, Tristan's guitar whispered a melody—an ethereal composition that seemed to encapsulate the entirety of their love story. Marie-Élise's voice, though fragile, joined in, creating a harmonious duet that soared beyond the boundaries of human experience.

As the final chords faded into the room, they exchanged a knowing look—a gaze that conveyed a love that was timeless, boundless, and everlasting. Their love story had reached its earthly conclusion, but it was a narrative that would live eternally in the hearts of those who had been touched by their art, their music, and the profound connection they had shared.

And so, as they embraced the closing moments of their earthly voyage, they did so with the knowledge that their love was an eternal crescendo, a timeless masterpiece painted with the colours of their hearts, a symphony that would continue to resonate in the hearts of all who had been privileged to witness the beauty of their love. It was a love story that would endure through the ages, an everlasting reminder of the enduring power of passion, creativity, and a love that transcended the boundaries of time and space—a love that would forever compose the verses of eternity.

Chapter 35: The Endless Love

In the soft twilight of their lives, Tristan and Marie-Élise ventured into the final chapter of their extraordinary love story, a narrative painted with the vibrant strokes of passion, artistry, and an unbreakable bond that had defied the constraints of time. As they stood on the precipice of eternity, their love remained an endless love, a flame that would forever illuminate the very essence of existence.

Their Vienna apartment, a sanctuary of cherished memories, seemed to exhale the very essence of a lifetime of love. It whispered tales of laughter that had once filled its rooms, the melodies spun from Tristan's guitar, and the canvases that had borne witness to Marie-Élise's creative brilliance. Every nook and cranny held the testimony of a love that had deepened with each passing day.

Though the years had left their mark on their bodies, their spirits remained unwavering. Tristan's aging fingers still danced gracefully across the strings of his guitar, conjuring melodies that narrated the epic of their enduring love. Marie-Élise's hands, though marked by time, continued to weave magic upon her canvases, capturing the very essence of love and beauty.

Their child, a living embodiment of their legacy, had become their steadfast support and protector. The bonds of family had deepened, a testament to the enduring love that had been the guiding star of their lives.

In the tranquil moments of their twilight, Tristan and Marie-Élise often sat together, their eyes communicating volumes that words could never capture. Their love had transcended the limitations of spoken language; it was a communion of souls that had found its sanctuary in the serene quietude of their shared existence.

One evening, bathed in the soft, golden embrace of the setting sun, Tristan's guitar whispered a melody—an ethereal composition that seemed to encapsulate the entirety of their love story, from its tender beginnings in Paris to its grand crescendo in Vienna. Marie-Élise's voice, though fragile, joined in, creating a harmonious duet that soared beyond the boundaries of human experience.

As the final chords faded into the room, they exchanged a knowing look—a gaze that conveyed a love that was timeless, boundless, and everlasting. Their love story had reached its earthly conclusion, but it was a narrative that would live eternally in the hearts of those who had been touched by their art, their music, and the profound connection they had shared.

And so, as they embraced the closing moments of their earthly voyage, they did so with the knowledge that their love was an endless love, a timeless masterpiece painted with the colours of their hearts, a symphony that would continue to resonate in the hearts of all who had been privileged to witness the beauty of their love. It was a love story that would endure through the ages, an everlasting reminder of the enduring power of passion, creativity, and a love that transcended the boundaries of time and space—a love that would forever write the eternal verses of existence itself.

Conclusion: Love's Eternal Legacy

In the twilight of their lives, Tristan and Marie-Élise's extraordinary love story came to a close, leaving behind a legacy that would endure through the ages. Their journey, painted with the vivid hues of passion, creativity, and an unbreakable connection, had transcended the boundaries of time and space. It was a testament to the enduring power of love—a love that defied the constraints of mortality and resonated with a timeless, boundless, and everlasting essence.

Their Vienna apartment, a sanctuary of cherished memories, remained a silent witness to the symphony of their love. It echoed with the laughter that had once filled its rooms, the melodies spun from Tristan's guitar, and the canvases that had borne witness to Marie-Élise's creative brilliance. Every corner whispered the tale of a love that had deepened with each passing day.

As the years etched their presence upon their bodies, Tristan and Marie-Élise's spirits remained unyielding. Tristan's aging fingers continued to caress the strings of his guitar, conjuring melodies that narrated the epic of their enduring love. Marie-Élise's hands, marked by time, continued to weave magic upon her canvases, capturing the very essence of love and beauty.

Their child, the living embodiment of their legacy, had become their steadfast support and protector. The bonds of family had deepened, reflecting the enduring love that had guided their lives.

In the tranquil moments of their twilight, Tristan and Marie-Élise often sat together, their eyes communicating volumes that words could never encapsulate. Their love had transcended the limitations of spoken language; it was a communion of souls that had found its sanctuary in the serene quietude of their shared existence.

Their love story, like an eternal melody, had reached its earthly conclusion, but it would live on eternally in the hearts of those who had been touched by their art, their music, and the profound connection they had shared. It was a love story that defied time and space, a timeless masterpiece painted with the colours of their hearts, a symphony that would continue to resonate in the hearts of all who had been privileged to witness the beauty of their love.

And so, as they embraced the closing moments of their earthly voyage, they did so with the knowledge that their love was an endless legacy, a love that would forever inspire, uplift, and remind the world of the enduring power of passion, creativity, and a love that transcended the boundaries of mortality. Their love had become a part of the very fabric of existence, a testament to the eternal nature of love itself—a love that would forever echo in the hearts and souls of all who dared to believe in its enduring magic.

Closing Notes by Author
Laurie Ravello

As we come to the final chords of "The French Affair," I am deeply grateful for the privilege of sharing this journey of love, passion, and artistry with you, cherished readers. It has been an extraordinary odyssey, one that has resonated in the hearts of many, and for that, I thank you from the depths of my creative soul.

"The French Affair" is more than just a story; it is a testament to the enduring power of love and the transformative nature of art. Through the streets of Paris and the alleys of Vienna, through the strokes of Marie-Élise's brush and the melodies of Tristan's guitar, we have explored the intricate dance between creativity and the human heart. We have witnessed how two souls, seemingly worlds apart, can converge and create a love that defies time and distance.

As an author, my greatest joy has been in crafting a narrative that speaks to the profound emotions that connect us all—love, longing, inspiration, and the pursuit of our truest passions. I hope that, within these pages, you have found echoes of your own experiences and that you have been transported to a world where love and art hold sway.

My journey as an author is an ongoing endeavour, and your support and readership have been the wind beneath my wings. I encourage you to continue exploring the worlds of literature, to seek out stories that inspire and ignite your imagination, and to always believe in the magic of storytelling. For stories are the vessels through which we discover the complexities of the human experience, and in each tale, we find a piece of ourselves.

As we bid farewell to Tristan and Marie-Élise, may their love story remind you that the boundaries of love and creativity are boundless, and that the most beautiful symphonies are composed in the chambers of the heart. Until we meet again on the pages of another story, may your own life be filled with the melodies of love and the vibrant colours of passion.

With profound gratitude and warm regards,

Laurie Ravello

Don't miss out!

Visit the website below and you can sign up to receive emails whenever Laurie Ravello publishes a new book. There's no charge and no obligation.

https://books2read.com/r/B-A-LGLAB-TQKOC

BOOKS 2 READ

Connecting independent readers to independent writers.

About the Author

Author: Laurie Ravello

Laurie Ravello is an accomplished independent author celebrated for his exceptional talent in crafting stories that sweep readers off their feet and immerse them in the realms of love, romance, and profound discovery. With a remarkable ability to evoke powerful emotions and transport readers to captivating worlds, Laurie Ravello has become a literary force to be reckoned with.

Throughout his writing career, Laurie Ravello has demonstrated an innate gift for weaving intricate tales of love and romance that resonate deeply with readers. His narratives are known for their ability to take readers on emotional journeys, introducing them to characters whose experiences are both relatable and profoundly moving.

Laurie Ravello's works have earned acclaim for their vivid storytelling, rich character development, and the ability to explore the complexities of human emotions. Whether it's a tender love story, a passionate romance, or a narrative of self-discovery, Ravello's writing shines with authenticity and depth.

As an independent author, Laurie Ravello's dedication to his craft is evident in the way he meticulously constructs his stories. His narratives are often accompanied by beautifully descriptive prose that paints a vivid picture of the worlds he creates, allowing readers to fully immerse themselves in the story's settings and atmospheres.

With each new release, Laurie Ravello continues to captivate readers and earn their loyalty with his talent for crafting tales that touch the heart and soul. His work serves as an invitation to embark on journeys of love, passion, and self-discovery, leaving readers eagerly anticipating his next literary adventure.

Laurie Ravello's commitment to his craft and his ability to transport readers into the depths of love and romance have firmly established him as an independent author whose stories are cherished by those seeking narratives that both stir the emotions and provide an unforgettable literary experience.

Read more at joelravellobooks.shop.

Milton Keynes UK
Ingram Content Group UK Ltd.
UKHW040642061023
430068UK00001B/47